BIG HEAD

Esmeralda has magical powers – and she u... to teach the class big head a lesson!

Jean Ure was six when she wrote her first book and still at school when her first novel was published. Since then, she has written many popular titles for young people, including *A Proper Little Nooryeff*, *Whatever Happened to Katy-Jane?*, *The Unknown Planet*, *Captain Cranko and the Crybaby*, *Skinny Melon and Me*, *Becky Bananas*, *The Children Next Door* (shortlisted for the 1995 WH Smith Mind Boggling Books Award); and *A Twist in Time*. Her novel for young adults, *Plague 99*, was the 1991 Lancashire Children's Book of the Year. She lives in Surrey with her husband, dogs and cats.

Books by the same author

Captain Cranko and the Crybaby
The Unknown Planet

For older readers

A Twist in Time
Whatever Happened to Katy-Jane?

JEAN URE

BIG HEAD

Illustrations by Mike Gordon

WALKER BOOKS
AND SUBSIDIARIES

LONDON • BOSTON • SYDNEY

First published 1999 by
Walker Books Ltd, 87 Vauxhall Walk
London SE11 5HJ

This edition published 2002

2 4 6 8 10 9 7 5 3 1

Text © 1999 Jean Ure
Illustrations © 1999 Mike Gordon

This book has been typeset in Garamond

Printed and bound in Great Britain by The Guernsey Press Co. Ltd

British Library Cataloguing in Publication Data:
a catalogue record for this book is
available from the British Library

ISBN 0-7445-8986-X

CONTENTS

TROUBLE!

Esmeralda was in trouble. *Again.*
She had turned Darren Hopgood
into a frog.

"Why did you do it?" wailed her
mum.

"I had to teach him a lesson," said
Esmeralda. "He'd got this frog and
he was going to chop off its legs
and eat them."

Her mum couldn't understand why she hadn't just taken the frog away from him, but Esmeralda explained: she had wanted him to know how it *felt* to be a frog, and to be frightened.

"You always told me," said Esmeralda, "that if a person had magical powers they had to do good with them."

Her mum sighed. Esmeralda meant well, there was no doubt about that. But, oh dear! The problems she caused. Now they would have to pack their bags and go flying off all over again. Never in one place for more than five seconds! It was *so* unsettling.

"I'd become quite fond of Brighton," said Esmeralda's mum.

All through the summer,
Esmeralda's mum had sat in her
little striped tent on the sea front.
People came from far and wide to
cross her palm with silver and hear
what the future had in store.

And Esmeralda's mum had gazed into her crystal ball and told them all the good things that were going to happen.

Sometimes she warned them of bad things.

Everyone knew Madame Petulengro. She was the best fortune teller for miles around!

And now Esmeralda had gone and turned a boy into a frog and the news was bound to leak out. News always did.

Trouble, trouble! Esmeralda's mum picked up her crystal ball and dumped it into a Sainsbury's carrier bag. Nothing but trouble!

Esmeralda shuffled uncomfortably. "I'm sorry, Mum!"

But she had only done what had to be done. At least Darren Hopgood would never be cruel to a frog again.

UP AND AWAY

That night, Esmeralda and her mum flew out of Brighton on their magic carpet.

They had to fly at night. If they flew in the daytime people stood and stared and went, "Ooh, look at that! A flying carpet!"

"Where are we going this time?"
said Esmeralda, bouncing.

"Wherever the carpet takes us,"
snapped her mum. "And just stop
bouncing!"

Really, all this flying about was
such a nuisance!

They floated on, across the night
sky; past the moon and through the
stars, over the rooftops, over the
treetops, until the first streaks of
dawn appeared in the sky – palest
pink, with rose-coloured fingers.
A good sign!

"Remember the rhyme?" said Esmeralda.

"Red sky at morn,
the world re-born;
Red sky at eve,
time to grieve."

Her mum just grunted.

At last they began to descend.

"Where are we?" squealed Esmeralda.

Madame Petulengro peered over the side. "Croydon Underpass," she said.

Croydon Underpass! Could anything be more exciting? Esmeralda giggled.

Her mum looked at her crossly. This was all Esmeralda's fault.

"Just be quiet," she said, "while I consult the crystal. Hm… I'm seeing a rather nice house with rooms to let in the centre of town. Let's go!"

The nice little house with rooms to let soon had a notice in one of its windows.

The crystal ball was on the table, the magic carpet rolled up in its corner. As for Esmeralda…

Her mum looked up, beaming, from the crystal.

"I've found just the school for you!"

The school was called Angel Road Juniors. It had a school uniform and a school motto: *Serve and Obey*.

"That means, *behave yourself*," said Esmeralda's mum. "Just remember…" She tapped a finger against the crystal ball. "I've got my eye on you!"

BRIAN BIG HEAD

Esmeralda was starting at her new school. Esmeralda had been to lots of new schools. This was because she just couldn't resist using her magical powers.

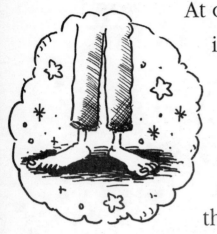

At one school, for instance, she had given the whole class two left feet. ("Because they were so horrid to this poor little boy who was a bit clumsy!")

At another school, she had given the prettiest girl in the class a nose like an old door knocker and made her teeth stick out. ("She was so vain, Mum!")

At yet another, she had turned her class teacher into a wart hog.

("He was really mean! He kept picking on people and making them cry.")

Esmeralda's teacher
at Angel Road was
called Miss Dainty.

"I won't turn *her*
into a wart hog," said
Esmeralda, earnestly.

From now on
she was going to
behave like a
normal schoolgirl.

"I promise!" said
Esmeralda.

Esmeralda tried.
She tried really hard.
But it was just *so-o-o*
difficult when you
had magical powers.

There was a boy in her class
called Brian Biggard. The other
children called him Brian Big Head.
Esmeralda soon discovered why.
Every time Miss Dainty asked a
question, Brian's hand shot up and
Brian's voice very loudly shouted
out the answer before anyone else
had a chance.

It was extremely annoying.
Esmeralda herself was bursting to
answer the questions.

But Brian always got in first. The
others didn't seem to care. They just
sat there like puddings. Didn't even
bother to try.

Jenna and Amy said there wasn't any point.

"That Big Head," said Amy. "He knows everything."

They were so used to Brian Big Head answering all the questions that it had made them stupid.

And yet they weren't really stupid! Esmeralda was going to have to take some action here. Put her magical powers to good use!

She turned, and let her eyes bore into the back of Brian's head. Just imagine if lots of little holes appeared and all his brains started leaking out…

A voice spoke sharply in Esmeralda's head. *What are you up to?*

Bother! Esmeralda started, guiltily.

That was the trouble with having a mum like Esmeralda's. She could glance into her crystal ball at any moment and catch you doing something you shouldn't. She could even get inside your head and read your thoughts. And Brian Big Head was *still* answering all the questions!

It was so unfair.

"Life is like that," said Jenna.

"You just have to put up with it," said Amy.

But Esmeralda tossed her head. Amy and Jenna might put up with it. She wasn't going to!

MORE TROUBLE

Esmeralda's mum was going up to town for the day. And guess what? She was leaving her crystal ball behind!

That meant that she couldn't look into it and see what Esmeralda was up to…

This was Esmeralda's chance. The time had come to teach Brian Big Head a thing or two!

She waited until the first lesson
after break. And *then*…

Something very strange began to happen. Brian's head began to swell! It swelled and it swelled until

it was the size of a football … .

the size of a pumpkin …

the size of a great gas-filled
balloon and growing even bigger!

The rest of the class sat staring
in amazement. One or two of them
giggled.

The only person who didn't
seem to notice was Miss Dainty.
Maybe that had something to do
with Esmeralda.

"Who can
answer question
number four?"
said Miss Dainty.

"Question
number five?"

"Question
number six?"

It was time someone else had a go. Esmeralda didn't want to be as big-headed as Brian (who by now was *very* big-headed indeed).

She waited.
But nothing
happened.
Well, go on!
thought Esmeralda.
What was the
matter with these
people? She had
silenced Brian Big
Head for them!
Maybe they
needed teaching
a lesson too…

Slowly, slowly, all around the room, heads started to shrink.

They shrank to grapefruit …

shrank to tennis balls …

shrank to hazelnuts …

shrank to – pin-heads!

Twenty-four children, with heads
so tiny they could scarcely be seen.
"Look at Robert!" giggled Jenna.
Then she looked at Amy and her
jaw dropped. But only by a
millimetre, because now she was

a pin-head! Then Amy looked at
Jenna, and her eyes grew wide.
But only as wide as a micro-dot,
because she was a pin-head, too!

They were *all* pin-heads! The
whole lot of them.

Except of course, for Brian.
Brian was a *balloon head*.

And still Miss Dainty didn't notice. "Esmeralda?" she beamed.

CAUGHT!

"Hey, deary me! How tired I be,"
sighed Madame Petulengro.

Now there was going to be
trouble! Madame Petulengro had
come home! *Early*.

She yawned and pulled the crystal ball towards her. What was this she saw? A class full of children with tiny heads (all except for one boy, who had a head like a giant puff ball). And in the midst of them, grinning triumphantly…

Esmeralda!

Drat that girl! She was up to her tricks again.

"You come home this instant!" shrieked Madame Petulengro. *"And put those children back the way you found them!"*

"Oh, if I must," sighed Esmeralda.

Miss Dainty turned
from the board. She
looked across with
a smile to where
Esmeralda had been
sitting.

"Three times
seventeen. Es—"
Her voice faded. She looked
puzzled. Which child
had she been going
to ask? Her eye fell
on a small rabbity-
faced girl sucking
her thumb.

"Esther?" said
Miss Dainty.

And Esther,
who hadn't
answered
a question for
so long that
no one could
remember, took
her thumb out
of her mouth
and said,
"Fifty-one."

Which was,
of course,
quite correct.
Miss Dainty
could hardly
believe it!

"Question number seven?" she said.

Brian's hand went shooting up. So did Esther's. So did Amy's. So did Jenna's, so did Robert's, so did Jonathan's. So did everyone's!

Miss Dainty blinked. Something very strange was going on in her class.

Yes! Thanks to Esmeralda and her magical powers, they had all woken up from a deep, deep sleep.

OFF WE GO AGAIN!

That night, Esmeralda and her mum packed their bags. *Again.* The crystal ball. The folding table. The special tablecloth covered in stars. The sign that said:

> MADAME PETULENGRO
> Horoscopes read
> Fortunes told

All packed up! All over again!

"Oh, why couldn't I have had a normal daughter?" sighed Esmeralda's mum.

"What cheek!" said Esmeralda. "How could you expect to have a normal daughter if you aren't a normal mum?"

Esmeralda's mum drew herself up, indignantly. "I am a perfectly normal mum," she said, stuffing her crystal ball into a Tesco carrier bag. "Get on that mat and let's go!"

They floated off, across the night sky. Past the moon and through the stars, over the rooftops and over the treetops.

"Where to this time?" wondered Esmeralda.

Wherever it was, it would be fun! Life was always fun when Esmeralda was around.

More ~~SPRINTERS~~ for you to enjoy!

- *Little Stupendo Flies High* Jon Blake — 0-7445-5970-7
- *Captain Abdul's Pirate School* Colin McNaughton — 0-7445-5242-7
- *The Ghost in Annie's Room* Philippa Pearce — 0-7445-5993-6
- *Molly and the Beanstalk* Pippa Goodhart — 0-7445-5981-2
- *Taking the Cat's Way Home* Jan Mark — 0-7445-8268-7
- *The Finger-eater* Dick King-Smith — 0-7445-8269-5
- *Care of Henry* Anne Fine — 0-7445-8270-9
- *Cup Final Kid* Martin Waddell — 0-7445-8297-0
- *Lady Long-legs* Jan Mark — 0-7445-8296-2
- *Posh Watson* Gillian Cross — 0-7445-8271-7
- *Impossible Parents* Brian Patten — 0-7445-9022-1
- *Patrick's Perfect Pet* Annalena McAfee — 0-7445-8911-8
- *Me and My Big Mouse* Simon Cheshire — 0-7445-5982-0
- *No Tights for George!* June Crebbin — 0-7445-5999-5
- *Big Head* Jean Ure — 0-7445-8986-X
- *The Magic Boathouse* Sam Llewellyn — 0-7445-8987-8
- *Easy Peasy* Sarah Hayes — 0-7445-9043-4
- *Art, You're Magic!* Sam McBratney — 0-7445-8985-1

All at £3.99